THE GRAPHIC
SHAKESPEARE SERIES

MACBETH

Published by
Evans Brothers Limited
2A Portman Mansions
Chiltern Street
London W1M 1LE

© in the modern text Hilary Burningham 1997
© in the illustrations Evans Brothers Ltd 1997
Designed by Design Systems Ltd.

British Library Cataloguing in Publication Data
Burningham, Hilary
   Macbeth. – (The Graphic Shakespeare series)
   1. Children's plays, English
   I. Title II. Lincoln, Charity III. Shakespeare, William, 1564-1616
   822.3'3

ISBN 0 237 51785 X

Printed in Hong Kong by Wing King Tong Co. Ltd.

THE GRAPHIC SHAKESPEARE SERIES

MACBETH

RETOLD BY HILARY BURNINGHAM
ILLUSTRATED BY CHARITY LINCOLN

EVANS BROTHERS LIMITED

THE CHARACTERS IN THE PLAY

Macbeth — Thane of Glamis, later of Cawdor, later King of Scotland

Lady Macbeth — wife of Macbeth

King Duncan — King of Scotland

Malcolm — son of King Duncan

Banquo — a Thane of Scotland

Macduff — a Thane of Scotland

Donalbain — son of King Duncan

Lennox — a Thane of Scotland

Ross — a Thane of Scotland

Lady Macduff — wife of Macduff

The Three Witches

The Porter

The Doctor

Hecat — another witch

PORTRAIT GALLERY

Macbeth

Lady Macbeth

King Duncan

Malcolm

Banquo

Macduff

Donalbain

Lennox

Ross

Lady Macduff

The 3 Witches

The Porter

The Doctor

Hecat

Macbeth

ACT 1

Three witches met on a rocky hill in Scotland.

It was a dark and stormy afternoon. There was thunder and lightning.

The witches were planning their next meeting. There was a battle going on. They wanted to meet after the battle, before the sun went down.

They planned to meet on the heath[1].

They wanted to meet a man called Macbeth.

[1]heath – a flat piece of land with no trees, only grass and small bushes

FIRST WITCH:	When shall we three meet again?
	In thunder, lightning, or in rain?
SECOND WITCH:	When the hurly-burly's done,
	When the battle's lost and won.
THIRD WITCH:	That will be ere the set of sun.
FIRST WITCH:	Where the place?
SECOND WITCH:	Upon the heath.
THIRD WITCH:	There to meet with Macbeth.

The battle was between the Scots and invaders[1] from Norway. A captain came from the battlefield. He was covered in blood.

Duncan, King of Scotland, and his two sons, Malcolm and Donalbain, wanted to hear about the battle. Were the Scots winning?

The captain told them that the Scots were winning. A brave Scotsman named Macbeth was leading the fight. He had killed the main enemy and cut off his head.

The King of Norway had come back with more soldiers. Macbeth and the other leader, Banquo, were not frightened. They fought twice as hard as before.

More messengers came from the battlefield. A Scottish thane[2], the Thane of Cawdor, had joined the Norwegians. He was a traitor[3] to King Duncan.

Macbeth and Banquo had fought bravely. They had won the battle.

King Duncan announced that the Thane of Cawdor must die. Macbeth was the new Thane of Cawdor.

[1]invaders – people who want to take over someone else's land or country
[2]thane – a special title like Lord or Sir
[3]traitor – someone who does not support the king

KING: What bloody man is that? He can report,
As seemeth by his plight, of the revolt
The newest state.

The three witches met on the heath. They joined hands and danced in a circle.

They heard a drum in the distance. Macbeth and Banquo were coming!

The first witch spoke to Macbeth by his title, Thane of Glamis. There was nothing unusual in that. Macbeth was the Thane of Glamis.

The next witch called Macbeth "Thane of Cawdor".

The last witch said that Macbeth would one day be king.

Then Banquo asked the witches about his future. The witches said Banquo would not be king, but his children would be kings.

Macbeth knew that the Thane of Cawdor was still alive. King Duncan was alive and had sons of his own. What were the witches talking about?

The witches vanished[1].

[1]vanished – suddenly could not be seen

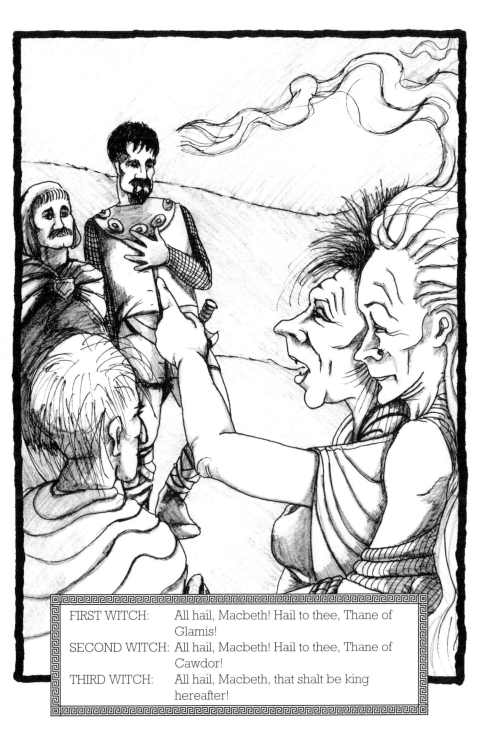

FIRST WITCH: All hail, Macbeth! Hail to thee, Thane of
                  Glamis!
SECOND WITCH: All hail, Macbeth! Hail to thee, Thane of
                  Cawdor!
THIRD WITCH: All hail, Macbeth, that shalt be king
                  hereafter!

At that moment, Ross and Angus, messengers from King Duncan, appeared. King Duncan had said Cawdor must die because he had fought on the side of the King of Norway. Macbeth was to have his title, Thane of Cawdor.

The second witch's saying had come true.

ROSS: And, for an earnest of a greater honour,
             He bade me from him call thee Thane of Cawdor
             In which addition, hail, most worthy thane,
             For it is thine.
BANQUO: What! Can the devil speak true?
MACBETH: The Thane of Cawdor lives. Why do you dress
             me
             In borrowed robes?

Macbeth started to think about becoming king. If he was to be king, other people must die. He had evil thoughts. He was frightened by his own thoughts.

What would he have to do to make the third witch's saying come true?

Perhaps the third witch's saying would come true even if he did nothing.

MACBETH: *(aside)* If chance will have me king, why
chance may crown me
Without my stir.

BANQUO: New honours come upon him
Like our strange garments, cleave not to their
mould
But with the aid of use.

MACBETH: *(aside)* Come, what come may,
Time and the hour runs through the roughest
day.

Macbeth and Banquo went to meet King Duncan. The Thane of Cawdor was dead. Macbeth was the new Thane of Cawdor. He knelt in front of King Duncan. He promised to serve the King.

King Duncan praised Macbeth and Banquo for winning the battle.

King Duncan had an announcement. His eldest son, Malcolm, was to be the next king. He gave Malcolm the title, Prince of Cumberland.

This was not good news for Macbeth. He was starting to think about getting rid of Duncan and becoming king in his place. Now, Malcolm was to be the next king. There was another person in Macbeth's way.

King Duncan and his followers were to visit Macbeth's castle. Macbeth hurried back to get ready for the visit.

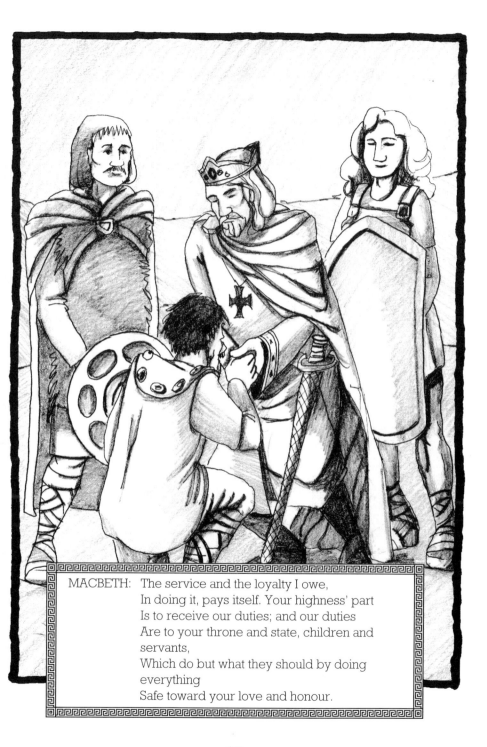

MACBETH: The service and the loyalty I owe,
           In doing it, pays itself. Your highness' part
           Is to receive our duties; and our duties
           Are to your throne and state, children and
           servants,
           Which do but what they should by doing
           everything
           Safe toward your love and honour.

Macbeth

At Macbeth's castle, his wife, Lady Macbeth, was
reading a letter from her husband. He told her about
the witches' prophecies[1]. They said he was Thane of
Cawdor. That turned out to be true. They said he
would be king. Would that come true as well?

Macbeth wanted to be king. Lady Macbeth wanted to
be queen. How badly did Macbeth want to be king?
Would he do evil deeds in order to become king?

A messenger came. King Duncan was on his way to
visit Macbeth's castle. Lady Macbeth saw that they
had the chance to get rid of King Duncan. She had to
make sure that Macbeth would do the murder. She
called on all the evil spirits to make her strong.

She didn't even want a mother's milk in her breasts.
She wanted gall[2]!

[1]prophecies – messages about what will happen in the future
[2]gall – a bitter juice

LADY MACBETH: The raven himself is hoarse
That croaks the fatal entrance of Duncan
Under my battlements. Come, you spirits
That tend on mortal thoughts, unsex me here
And fill me from the crown to the toe top-full
Of direst cruelty.

Macbeth came home. He and Lady Macbeth talked about King Duncan's visit. He would stay for only one night. Macbeth had to make up his mind.

King Duncan had to be murdered that night. Lady Macbeth was sure about that. She told Macbeth not to let his feelings show. He had to be a good host[1]. His royal guests should have a proper welcome. He must smile and be very friendly, even though he was planning to kill Duncan.

Macbeth was not yet sure about murdering the king. He wanted to talk about it later.

[1]host – a person who receives people in his own home

LADY MACBETH: Your face, my thane, is as a book where men
May read strange matters. To beguile the time
Look like the time, bear welcome in your eye,
Your hand, your tongue; look like the innocent
flower,
But be the serpent under't.

Lady Macbeth greeted the king, his sons, and all his followers, Banquo and the rest. They were all happy to be at Macbeth's castle. They said it was a very pleasant place. They enjoyed the fresh air.

Lady Macbeth was good at following her own advice. She welcomed them to the castle. She was pleasant and smiling. No one had any idea that she was making evil plans.

LADY MACBETH: All our service
In every point twice done and then done double
Were poor and single business to contend
Against those honours deep and broad wherewith
Your majesty loads our house.

Macbeth

Macbeth still couldn't make up his mind about killing King Duncan.

If Macbeth became king by doing murder, someone might then murder him.

King Duncan felt safe at Macbeth's castle. He was Macbeth's king, King of Scotland. He was a visitor in Macbeth's house.

King Duncan was a good, wise king. That was another reason not to kill him.

Macbeth decided not to kill King Duncan after all. At that moment, Lady Macbeth came looking for him. Macbeth told her he had decided not to kill the king.

Lady Macbeth was very angry.

She told Macbeth that he didn't love her. She said that he wasn't a real man. She said that she would never change her mind as Macbeth had done.

She promised Macbeth that they wouldn't be found out. Two servants slept near King Duncan. She would give them lots of wine. Macbeth could smear the servants with Duncan's blood. Everyone would think the servants had done the murder.

She convinced Macbeth. He changed his mind again. He would kill King Duncan.

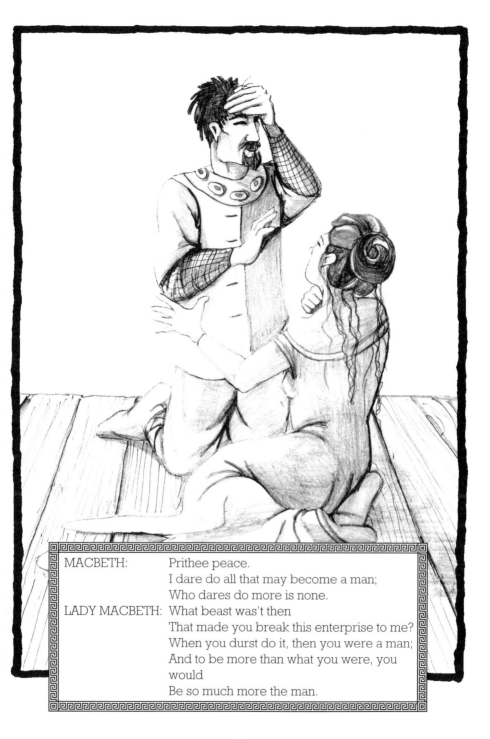

MACBETH: Prithee peace.
I dare do all that may become a man;
Who dares do more is none.
LADY MACBETH: What beast was't then
That made you break this enterprise to me?
When you durst do it, then you were a man;
And to be more than what you were, you
would
Be so much more the man.

ACT 2

Macbeth had decided to kill King Duncan. He thought he could see a dagger hanging in front of his eyes. Was he imagining it? The dagger changed. It dripped with blood. Macbeth knew it wasn't real.

Lady Macbeth had given the servants a lot of wine. They were asleep.

It was time for Macbeth to go and murder King Duncan.

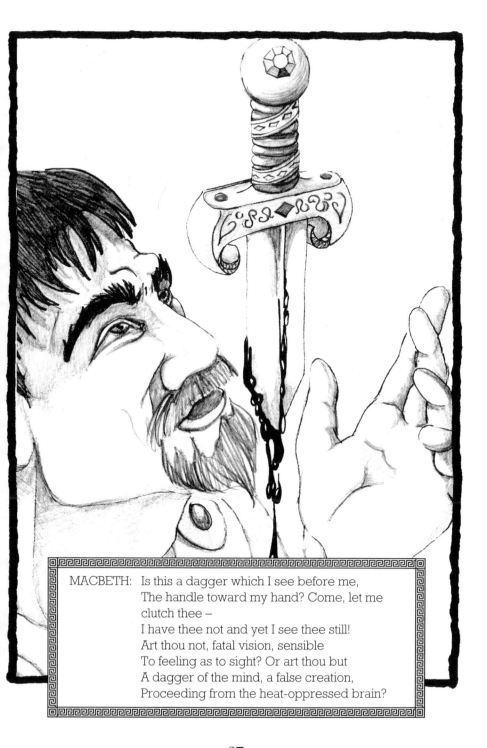

MACBETH: Is this a dagger which I see before me,
The handle toward my hand? Come, let me
clutch thee –
I have thee not and yet I see thee still!
Art thou not, fatal vision, sensible
To feeling as to sight? Or art thou but
A dagger of the mind, a false creation,
Proceeding from the heat-oppressed brain?

Lady Macbeth gave the two servants drugs as well as wine.

Macbeth murdered King Duncan with the servants' daggers. He took the daggers away with him. He should have left them near the servants.

Lady Macbeth told him to take the daggers back and smear the servants with King Duncan's blood. Macbeth was afraid to go back. He didn't want to think about what he had done.

Lady Macbeth took the daggers from him. Quickly, she put the daggers near the servants. She smeared King Duncan's blood all over them. Everyone would think that the servants had murdered Duncan.

Someone was knocking at the castle gates. Macbeth and Lady Macbeth went to wash the blood off their hands and put on their nightclothes. It would look odd if they were still dressed in the middle of the night.

It would be easy to wash the blood off their hands – so Lady Macbeth thought.

LADY MACBETH: Why did you bring these daggers from the place?
They must lie there. Go, carry them and smear
The sleepy grooms with blood.

MACBETH: I'll go no more.
I am afraid to think what I have done;
Look on't again I dare not.

LADY MACBETH: Infirm of purpose!
Give me the daggers.

Early in the morning, two Thanes, Macduff and
Lennox, arrived at Macbeth's castle. A porter came to
the door. He had been drinking the night before.
Macduff was making jokes with him. No one knew
that anything was wrong. No one knew that the king
was dead.

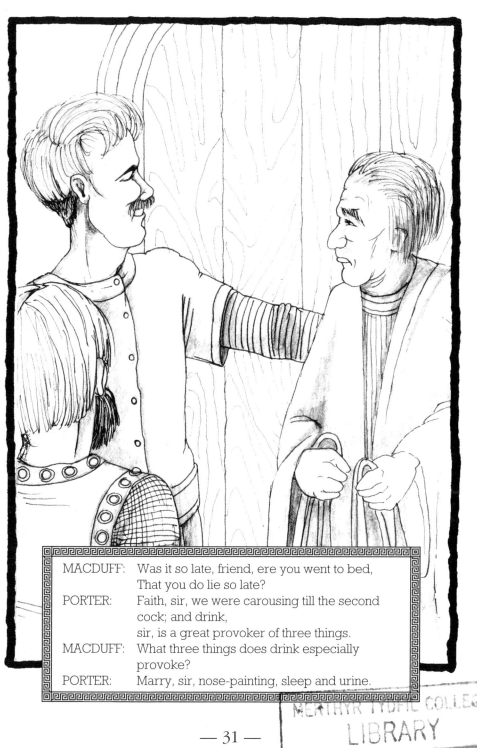

MACDUFF: Was it so late, friend, ere you went to bed,
          That you do lie so late?
PORTER: Faith, sir, we were carousing till the second
          cock; and drink,
          sir, is a great provoker of three things.
MACDUFF: What three things does drink especially
          provoke?
PORTER: Marry, sir, nose-painting, sleep and urine.

Macbeth

Macbeth showed Macduff where King Duncan was 'sleeping'. Macduff went to wake him up.

Macduff came back. He was full of horror. The king was dead. He was lying murdered in his bed.

Soon, all the others came to hear the terrible news. First, Lady Macbeth and Banquo, then Lennox and Ross, finally, Malcolm and Donalbain, the king's sons.

Who could have done such a terrible deed? Lennox and Macbeth had been to have a look. Lennox said that the servants had bloody daggers beside them. Their clothes and faces were covered with blood. The servants must have murdered the king.

Macbeth told them that the servants were not sleeping. The servants were dead. Duncan's body had awful stab wounds and both the servants were covered with blood. He couldn't help it, he said. He had to kill them.

Lady Macbeth fainted and had to be taken away.

Malcolm and Donalbain were not happy with all these murders. They were not happy with the reasons they heard. They decided to go away. Malcolm went to England. Donalbain went to Ireland. They would feel safer away from Scotland – and Macbeth.

LADY MACBETH: *(fainting)* Help me hence, ho!
MACDUFF: Look to the lady!
MALCOLM: *(to Donalbain)* Why do we hold our tongues,
That most may claim this argument for ours?
DONALBAIN: *(to Malcolm)* What should be spoken here where our fate,
Hid in an auger-hole, may rush and seize us?
Let's away. Our tears are not yet brewed.

Ross was talking to an old man. Strange things were happening. Although it was daytime, everywhere was dark.

A falcon[1] had been killed by an owl[2]. Owls usually killed mice.

King Duncan's beautiful horses broke out of their stalls and ate each other.

Everything was against nature.

Macduff came with more news. Malcolm and Donalbain had run away. Now, everyone thought they had killed their father, King Duncan. With them out of the way, Macbeth was the new king. He was to be crowned at Scone.

Macduff didn't want to go to Scone. Would Macbeth be a good king, as Duncan had been?

[1]falcon – bird that hunts other birds and small animals, during the day
[1]owl – bird that hunts small animals, at night

MACDUFF: Malcolm and Donalbain, the King's two sons,
          Are stolen away and fled, which puts upon them
          Suspicion of the deed.

ACT 3

Macbeth was now King of Scotland. Banquo was thinking about the witches' sayings. All the things they had said to Macbeth had come true. First, he became Thane of Cawdor, then King of Scotland. Banquo had an idea that Macbeth had done bad deeds to become king.

The witches had told Banquo that his children would be kings of Scotland. Would that prophecy come true?

Macbeth and Lady Macbeth (now the king and queen) invited Banquo to a grand banquet that evening. Banquo and his son, Fleance, were going out for a ride in the afternoon. Macbeth asked a lot of questions about where they planned to go.

When he was alone, Macbeth thought about Banquo. Macbeth was now king, but was he safe on the throne while Banquo was alive? The witches told Banquo that his children would be kings. Had Macbeth killed King Duncan and his servants so that Banquo's children could be kings?

MACBETH: Here's our chief guest.
LADY MACBETH: If he had been forgotten
                It had been as a gap in our great feast
                And all-thing unbecoming.

Macbeth met with two men. He explained why they should kill Banquo.

The men didn't care about the reasons. They were murderers. They said they would kill Banquo.

Macbeth said he would send someone to tell them where Banquo would be. Also, at the same time, they had to kill Fleance, Banquo's son.

The murderers agreed.

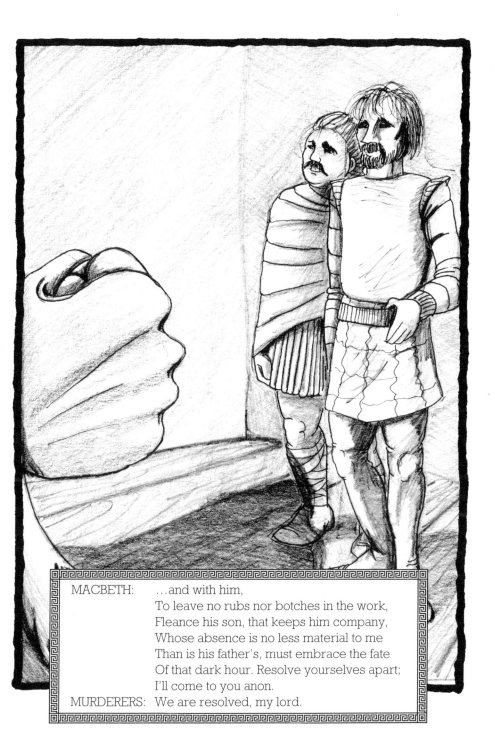

MACBETH: …and with him,
To leave no rubs nor botches in the work,
Fleance his son, that keeps him company,
Whose absence is no less material to me
Than is his father's, must embrace the fate
Of that dark hour. Resolve yourselves apart;
I'll come to you anon.
MURDERERS: We are resolved, my lord.

Macbeth and Lady Macbeth talked together. They were not happy. They were having terrible nightmares[1] every night.

Macbeth had done the murders to become king. Now, he didn't feel safe or happy.

Macbeth pretended that Banquo was coming to the banquet that night. Macbeth knew that Banquo and Fleance were going to be murdered.

Macbeth almost told Lady Macbeth that Banquo was to be murdered. In the end, he didn't. It was better if she didn't know there was to be another murder.

[1]nightmares – very bad dreams

LADY MACBETH: How now, my lord? Why do you keep alone,
Of sorriest fancies your companions making,
Using those thoughts which should indeed have died
With them they think on? Things without all remedy
Should be without regard; what's done is done.

MACBETH: We have scorched the snake, not killed it;
She'll close and be herself, whilst our poor malice
Remains in danger of her former tooth.

There were three murderers. Macbeth had sent the third murderer to show the way.

Banquo and Fleance came back from their ride. They were walking their horses back to the castle. Fleance carried a torch. The murderers attacked them.

Banquo was killed. The torch went out. In the dark, Fleance managed to escape.

SECOND MURDERER:	A light, a light!
THIRD MURDERER:	'Tis he.
FIRST MURDERER:	Stand to't!
BANQUO:	It will be rain tonight.
FIRST MURDERER:	Let it come down!

Macbeth

The great lords and ladies of Scotland came to Macbeth's banquet that night. He was their king. He should have had a wonderful time. He didn't.

One of the murderers came in. Macbeth left his seat to speak with the murderer. The murderer had blood on his face – Banquo's blood. Banquo was dead, but Fleance had escaped. Macbeth still could not feel safe.

Macbeth returned to his seat. But what was this? The ghost of Banquo, blood on his hair, face, everywhere, was sitting in Macbeth's place! Macbeth spoke to the ghost. No one else at the banquet could see it. They thought Macbeth was ill.

Lady Macbeth pretended everything was alright. She couldn't see Banquo's ghost. Macbeth was very frightened. She told him to pull himself together.

At last, the ghost disappeared. Macbeth tried to make excuses for his strange actions.

Lady Macbeth told everyone to leave. The banquet was over.

There was something else to worry about. Macbeth had sent for Macduff. Macduff refused to come.

Macbeth wanted to speak to the witches again. Everything was going wrong. Perhaps they would help him.

MACBETH: Thou canst not say I did it; never shake
Thy gory locks at me.

Again, the witches met on the heath. Hecat joined them. She was the chief of all the witches.

Hecat was angry. The witches had been dealing with Macbeth on their own. They should have asked her advice. Macbeth was an evil, weak man. They had wasted their magic on him.

Hecat knew that Macbeth was getting deeper and deeper into trouble. He would soon try to find the witches. She told them to make sure that he came to a final, bad end.

HECAT: How did you dare
To trade and traffic with Macbeth
In riddles and affairs of death,
And I, the mistress of your charms,
The close contriver of all harms
Was never called to bear my part,
Or show the glory of our art?

The Scottish lords knew that Macbeth was evil. The murders, the bloodshed[1], were pulling Scotland down. The lords were afraid of Macbeth. They were afraid to speak.

Lennox and another lord had a quiet chat. There was some hopeful news. Malcolm, son of King Duncan, had gone to the English court. There, Edward, King of England, had given him a safe place. Macduff had also gone to England. He was trying to get help to fight Macbeth. Macbeth had heard about these plans. He was getting ready to fight back.

Beautiful Scotland was suffering with Macbeth as king. Everyone was praying that he would soon be beaten. Scotland would be peaceful again.

[1]bloodshed – killing, spilling blood

LORD: Thither Macduff
Is gone to pray the holy king, upon his aid,
To wake Northumberland and warlike Seyward,
That by the help of these – with Him above
To ratify the work – we may again
Give to our tables meat, sleep to our nights,
Free from our feasts and banquets bloody knives,
Do faithful homage and receive free honours –

ACT 4

The witches were again on the heath. They had a huge cauldron[1]. They were throwing all kinds of horrible things into the cauldron. The cauldron helped their magic.

Something wicked was near. Macbeth was coming.

This time, with the help of the magic cauldron, the witches showed Macbeth some visions .

First, there was a soldier's head. It told Macbeth to be careful of Macduff.

Next, there was a child, covered in blood. It told Macbeth that no one born of woman could hurt him.

The third vision was a child wearing a crown and holding a tree in his hand. It told Macbeth that he would never be beaten until Birnan Wood came to Dunsinane Hill. Macbeth's castle was at Dunsinane Hill. How could a forest walk up a hill?

Lastly, Macbeth asked the witches if Banquo's children would be kings of Scotland. The witches showed him Banquo and a line of kings – eight of them. The last king had a mirror in his hand.

Macbeth was upset by the vision of Banquo and the kings. The witches laughed at him and disappeared.

[1]cauldron – a large pot for boiling

MACBETH: ...the eighth appears, who bears a glass
Which shows me many more. And some I see
That two-fold balls and treble sceptres carry.
Horrible sight! Now I see 'tis true,
For the blood-boltered Banquo smiles upon me,
And points at them for his. What! Is this so?

Lennox brought bad news to Macbeth. Macduff had gone to England.

Macbeth was angry. He decided to send soldiers to Macduff's castle. He would tell them to kill Macduff's family. More murders. This time it was to be Macduff's wife and all his children.

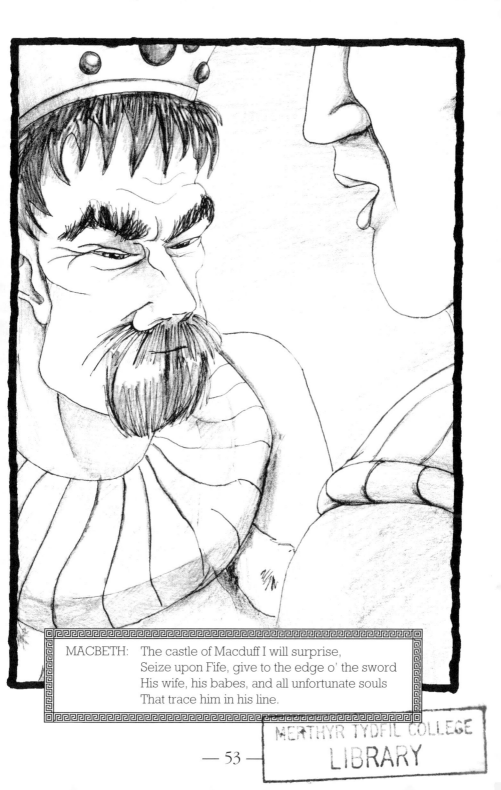

MACBETH: The castle of Macduff I will surprise,
Seize upon Fife, give to the edge o' the sword
His wife, his babes, and all unfortunate souls
That trace him in his line.

Ross went to Macduff's castle to see Lady Macduff. He told her that Macduff had escaped to England. She was very angry. Macduff had left her and the children in danger. No one was safe in Scotland in these times. Before he left, Ross told her that things would get better.

A messenger tried to tell Lady Macduff to escape with her children. It was too late. Macbeth's murderers were already there. Lady Macduff and all her children were horribly murdered.

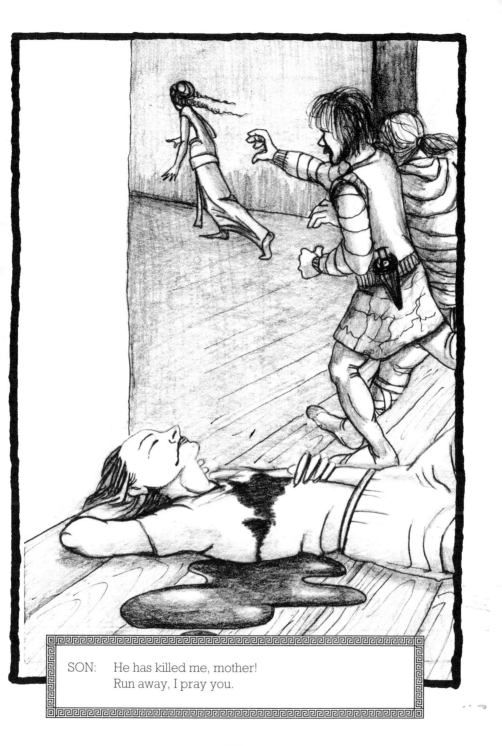

SON: He has killed me, mother!
Run away, I pray you.

Macbeth

Malcolm and Macduff met in England.

Macbeth was so evil that no one trusted anyone else. Malcolm was afraid that Macduff had come to harm him. He thought Macduff might be working for Macbeth. He pretended that he didn't want to be king. He told Macduff about all his bad points. He was really testing Macduff.

At last, Malcolm realised that Macduff wasn't working for Macbeth. Macduff also hated Macbeth and wanted to get rid of him. They both wanted to save Scotland from Macbeth. Malcolm wanted to be king. The English were giving him ten thousand men to help fight Macbeth. He and Macduff would fight Macbeth together.

A doctor came, talking about the English king. The king was a very religious man. He was able to make sick people better. How different from Macbeth. He was a killer and a murderer. Poor Scotland.

Ross arrived from Scotland with very bad news for Macduff. Lady Macduff and all her children were dead – murdered. Macduff felt terrible. It was all his fault.

He swore to get revenge on Macbeth. He and Malcolm would fight together. There would be no escape for Macbeth!

MACDUFF: Front to front
Bring thou this fiend of Scotland and myself.
Within my sword's length set him; if he scape,
Heaven forgive him too.

ACT 5

At Macbeth's castle, Lady Macbeth's servant was worried about her mistress. She was walking in her sleep. The servant didn't know what to do. She asked the doctor to come. Together, they watched Lady Macbeth.

She walked with her eyes wide open. She wasn't seeing anything. All the time, she was trying to wash her hands. She thought her hands were covered with blood. She couldn't get the blood off her hands. She talked about all Macbeth's murders. She talked about King Duncan, Macduff's wife and children, and Banquo.

She thought she was talking to Macbeth. She told him that Banquo couldn't come out of his grave.

The servant took Lady Macbeth back to bed. The doctor felt very sorry for Lady Macbeth. There was nothing he could do for her.

LADY MACBETH: Out, damned spot! Out, I say! – One: two: why then, 'tis time to do't. – Hell is murky! – Fie , my lord, fie! A soldier and afeard? – What need we fear who knows it, when none can call our power to accompt? – Yet who would have thought the old man to have had so much blood in him?

The armies were gathering to fight Macbeth. They were all to meet at Birnan Wood, not far from Macbeth's castle of Dunsinane.

Macbeth was trying to make his castle strong. Some thought he was mad. Some thought he was brave. Everyone hated him.

MENTETH: What does the tyrant?
CATHNESS: Great Dunsinane he strongly fortifies.
Some say he's mad. Others, that lesser hate him,
Do call it valiant fury; but for certain
He cannot buckle his distempered cause
Within the belt of rule.

At Dunsinane, Macbeth was told about the huge English army. Ten thousand soldiers had come to fight against him. The battle hadn't started, but he shouted for his armour. He said he would fight until he was hacked to bits.

He spoke to the doctor about Lady Macbeth. She was ill, but the illness was in her mind. She was thinking about all the evil things that Macbeth had done. She couldn't sleep. The doctor could do nothing to help her.

Even though the English soldiers were helping the Scots, Macbeth felt safe. The trees of Birnan Wood couldn't come marching to Dunsinane, could they?

MACBETH: How does your patient, doctor?
DOCTOR: Not so sick, my lord,
As she is troubled with thick-coming fancies
That keep her from her rest.
MACBETH: Cure her of that.
Canst thou not minister to a mind diseased,
Pluck from the memory a rooted sorrow,
Raze out the written troubles of the brain…?

Malcolm and Macduff and all their soldiers came to Birnan Wood. Malcolm had a good idea. The soldiers must each cut down a large branch and carry it in front of them. Macbeth, looking out from the castle, would not know how many soldiers were against him.

All the soldiers went to cut their branches. They would be good camouflage[1].

[1]camouflage – using natural shapes and colours to hide

MALCOLM: Let every soldier hew him down a bough
And bear't before him; thereby shall we shadow
The numbers of our host and make discovery
Err in report of us.

In his castle, Macbeth felt safe.

Suddenly, Lady Macbeth's servants cried out. Lady Macbeth was dead.

Macbeth was now alone. He felt empty. His life had no meaning. It had all been a waste of time.

A messenger brought frightening news. Birnan Wood was on the move. It was coming up the hill toward Dunsinane castle!

Macbeth remembered the witches' prophecy. He didn't know that 'Birnan Wood' was just the soldiers, carrying branches.

There was no point staying in his castle. He went out to fight his enemies. He would die with his armour on.

MACBETH: There is nor flying hence nor tarrying here.
          I 'gin to be aweary of the sun,
          And wish the estate o' the world were now
          undone –
          Ring the alarum bell! – Blow wind, come wrack,
          At least we'll die with harness on our back.

Macbeth

Macbeth fought young Seyward, an Englishman. He killed young Seyward. Macbeth was not afraid of anyone. Only someone who had not been born from a woman could hurt him. All people are born from a woman, their mother. Therefore, no one could hurt Macbeth, could they?

Malcolm and his lords were winning the battle. Macbeth's soldiers were leaving him. They were going over to Malcolm's side. The castle was taken without any fighting.

Macduff and Macbeth met. Macbeth didn't want to fight Macduff. But Macbeth's murderers had killed Macduff's wife and children. Macduff wanted revenge for the murder of his wife and children. They fought.

Macbeth boasted[1] about the witches' prophecy. He could not be hurt by anyone born of a woman. Macduff laughed. He was not born in the normal way. He had been taken from his mother's body. Macduff was not 'of woman born'. He and Macbeth were fighting to the death. Macbeth had no more prophecies left.

After a fierce fight, Macduff killed Macbeth.

[1]boasted – talked proudly

MACBETH: I bear a charmed life which must not yield
To one of woman born.
MACDUFF: Despair thy charm,
And let the angel whom thou still has served
Tell thee Macduff was from his mother's womb
Untimely ripped.

Malcolm and his lords had won the battle. Macduff came, holding Macbeth's head. Scotland was free again. The wicked king was dead.

Everyone shouted to Malcolm, "Hail, King of Scotland!"

Malcolm was to be crowned king at Scone. He invited all the people to come to his coronation.

MACDUFF: Hail, King! For so thou art. Behold where stands
The usurper's cursed head. The time is free.
I see thee compassed with thy kingdom's pearl
That speak my salutation in their minds,
Whose voices I desire aloud with mine. –
Hail, King of Scotland!